Lessons the Farmyard

by Emilie Poulsson

Christian Liberty Press

A PUBLICATION OF
Christian Liberty Press

© Copyright 1992
Christian Liberty Press
502 W. Euclid Avenue
Arlington Heights, Illinois 60004
USA

PREFACE

The love of animals is one of the most universal traits of early childhood. Instructors are encouraged to take advantage of this trait as they seek to impart important moral truths to children. The lessons contained in this text are designed to help parents and teachers minister to the spiritual needs of youngsters.

Instructors are advised to read the enclosed stories to the children that they are seeking to teach. It is very important to spend time discussing the lessons contained in each story with the children, both during and after each reading session. The teaching suggestions that are located at the back of this book provide creative ideas for sharing Biblical truths with young children. These suggestions will often provide the basis for profitable discussions regarding how to apply moral truth to everyday life.

May Almighty God use this book to strengthen and bless the lives of all of God's children.

Michael J. McHugh
Arlington Heights, Illinois
1993

TROTTINO.

HIS FAULTS.

There was once a mother-rabbit who had two little rabbit children. The older one was called Lapino and the other Trottino.

Lapino was a most lovable little rabbit. He was not only pretty, but good, also. Kind, obedient, good-humored, willing to give up to his little brother, and always ready to help his mother, Lapino was a model for all little rabbits.

His mamma would have been the happiest of rabbit-mothers if Trottino had been like his brother. But Trottino, though he was a very good little rabbit in many ways, had great faults.

He was disobedient, Trottino was; not from naughtiness, but because he did not try to think. When he wanted to do something which

he thought would be "good fun," he forgot all about his mother's wishes. If he had been more thoughtful he would have heard a voice, the voice of his little rabbit-conscience, saying to him, "Don't do that, Trottino! It is naughty!" But alas! he did not think of these things.

Another fault of Trottino's was greediness. He had a kind heart and would some-times go without a beautiful carrot, or a very tender cab-bage leaf, in order that he might give it to some poor lit-tle rabbit who had nothing to eat. But he was too fond of dainty food, and his mamma often tried to make him ashamed of it and sorry for it.

ASKING PARDON.

At such times he would throw himself on her neck

and ask her pardon, and say to her, "I won't do so any more!" But he would do the same thing the very next time.

He **did** not seem to know that a rabbit of honor ought to think well before giving his word, and that when his word was once given he ought to hold to it.

Lapino and Trottino began to be large enough to eat alone, but they did not yet know much about plants, and so their mother had told them not to eat anything unless she gave it to them.

When the weather was fine she took her children out for a walk in a beautiful field where there were all sorts of plants, and she pointed out to them which were good; but the rabbits were forbidden to go out into the field alone.

One morning Mother Rabbit saw that her cupboard was empty. She said to Lapino, " My little Lapino, I must go to the town. Hurry, my child! Get up, and make your bed and your little brother's, and have the room all clean and tidy

when I get home. I will come back as soon as I can, and take you out for a nice walk in the sun. You, Trottino, be good, and mind your brother."

" Yes, mamma," replied the two children ; and the mother

GOING TO MARKET.

rabbit, taking her big basket, hurried away.

Lapino arose. With his little paws he shook up the straw on which he had slept, and arranged it so that it had quite the air of a well-made bed.   Afterwards he carefully put the room in order.

Trottino did not usually trouble himself about such work, so Lapino was astonished to see him give all this help, and praised him for being kind and working well.

But if Trottino helped about

the house it was not for the sake of gaining compliments; he had another idea. When all the work was done he sat down in the open doorway of the house.

"Oh! do come and see, Lapino, how fine the weather is!" cried he to his brother.

"Very fine," answered Lapino; "when mamma comes home, and after she has taken a little rest, I shall be glad to go out of doors."

"Poor mamma! It is true that she will be very tired. She will have to rest a long while, and we shall have scarcely any time for our walk! What if it should rain?"

"That would be very provoking; but why do you think it will rain?"

"Because — because — I have heard Mr. Grisonnet, who is a very wise rabbit, say that when it is clear in the morning it often rains before night. It seems to me that there are clouds already! Come and see!"

Trottino slipped outside and went several steps away. Lapino followed him, but only as far as the door.

"I do not see any clouds," said he. "But where are you going, Trottino? Come back quickly! You know very well that we are not large enough to go out alone!"

"Oh! not last week, perhaps; but we have grown since then! My legs are stiff from staying in the house so long. I need to run."

"Oh, well! Run a little before the door, but do not go far."

"I do not know how to play all alone! I get tired of it! Dear Lapino, come; play with me. I will be good. I will not run away at all. If you knew how I long to play leap-frog!"

"COME, PLAY WITH ME. I WILL BE GOOD."

"Well, I'll come, then; but we must stay near the house," said Lapino.

So he went and played leap-frog; and he was thinking so

much of taking care of his little brother and keeping close to him, that he did not see how Trottino was gradually leading him farther and farther from home.

He stopped the game suddenly, however, because he found himself near a flight of steps which looked strange to him.

"Where have you brought me, Trottino?" said he, in an anxious tone. "We must go back home. What will mamma say if she does not find us there when she returns?"

"Bah! She won't say anything, because we will be there. Don't you see where our door is? It isn't far. We have still time to play; it isn't long since mamma went away. Oh! What beautiful lettuce! Surely that must be tender!"

There was, indeed, at the foot of the flight of steps, a basket full of lettuce. The woman who owned it had **gone** into the house to sell vegetables to the cook, and she had left her largest basket at the door while she went in. Trottino, greedy rascal, was nibbling as fast as he could at the best head of lettuce in her basket.

"Fie, Trottino! What are you doing there?" cried his brother. "If mamma should see you she would say that you were stealing, and that thieves deserved to go to prison between two policemen!"

"What crisp lettuce!" replied Trottino. "Mamma never brings us anything but the outside leaves; and the heart is the best part!"

As Trottino said this he received a kick which sent him rolling over toward his brother, while an angry voice called out:

"Wicked rabbit! A thief of a rabbit! Good only to be made into a stew!"

The woman who owned the vegetables had come out of the house and had seen him eating her lettuce. Of course she did not like that at all; and, as she had wooden shoes on, her kick pained Trottino very much, so that he ran away, groaning.

Lapino had not been kicked, but he was greatly frightened. The two children had now only one idea—to flee from the woman with the wooden shoes; and so in their terror they ran farther and farther still from home.

The poor little things ran so fast they were quite out of breath; but they did not dare stop an instant to rest. For whenever they looked back, as they did now and then, they saw the old woman, with the dreadful wooden shoe still thrust out.

They could hear her shouting, again and again, "Wicked rabbit! A thief of a rabbit! Good only to be made into a stew!" How angry she was!

How gladly would she have given Trottino another kick!

By and by her cry grew faint; then it ceased altogether. They turned a corner in the lane, and came to a wide green meadow. Their legs ached with running so fast and so far; and they had scarcely one bit of breath left.

FLEEING FROM THE WOMAN WITH WOODEN SHOES.

TROTTINO EATS THE POISONOUS HEMLOCK.

Lapino stopped first. "Where is our house now?" cried he, trembling.

"I don't know. Oh how she hurt me! that ugly woman!"

"See, Trottino; let us try to find our house again. Mamma will be so anxious! I believe it is on this side. You remember that big tree, don't you?"

"Yes! yes! Our house is right near the tree. We will be there very quickly; let me rest a little. Mamma has never brought us here."

"It is not prettier than our meadow, and there are plants growing here that we do not know."

"You — you do not know them; but I know them very well. Look! There is some wild thyme! That's something very delicious!"

"Yes, I believe it really is wild thyme; but mamma has

forbidden us to eat plants which she has not given us herself. You have had a good breakfast, Trottino. You do not need that wild thyme."

"I have breakfasted; but I have taken exercise since, so that I am now hungry again. Aren't you hungry, too?"

"Yes, I am hungry; but we must not disobey mamma. Let us go home quickly. Perhaps she has come back again, and then she will give us something to eat."

"Pretty soon. My paws are trembling. I have been so frightened! I shall have to eat a morsel to gain a little strength;" and Trottino, going into the grass still wet with dew, began to nibble the wild thyme.

Lapino shook his long ears with a troubled air. He would have liked to go back home and leave Trottino alone; but he stayed, thinking he could perhaps keep the giddy little fellow from doing more foolish and naughty things. He called to his brother every now and then, but Trottino was eating as fast as he could and would not stop.

Suddenly, however, he cried out: "Oh! Lapino! What beautiful parsley! I never saw any so large!"

"Are you quite sure that it *is* parsley? Parsley is not so tall."

"It is because this is unusually fine and good! Taste a little and you will see."

"I don't want to. It is wrong for you to eat it. Come, let's go."

"When I have had enough parsley. It is delicious!"

"Oh! Trottino! If mamma knew!"

"O, well! She won't know. At least, unless you are going to tell her, you horrid old tell-tale!"

"You know very well that I am not a tell-tale. But it is naughty to disobey. Do come, little brother."

"It is wrong for you to eat it. Come, let's go home."

He that covereth his sins shall not prosper:
but whoso confesseth and forsaketh
them shall have mercy.

PROVERBS 28:13

ΤROTTINO IS UN (—) ABLE TO EAT !

THE RETURN HOME.

Lapino looked so sad that Trottino was touched. "Very well," said he, "let's go home. Besides, I can't eat any more. What a pity! It was so good — that wild thyme — and that parsley!"

Lapino thought to himself that it was a very naughty thing to be greedy. Happily, Trottino was still young; there was hope that he might improve.

They had scarcely reached home when Mother Rabbit arrived. Lapino, who stood at the doorway, saw her coming.

"There is mamma!" he cried. "There is mamma, Trottino! Are you going to meet her?"

"I am tired. I am resting," replied Trottino in a weak voice.

"Oh! how you look! Are you sick, poor little fellow?"

"Why, no, indeed! A person can be tired without being sick, can't he? Don't tell mamma that I am sick, above all!"

Lapino said nothing, but went to meet Mother Rabbit, who kissed him and asked if he had been good.

"Very good, mamma," replied Lapino.

The mother rabbit also asked Trottino; who answered, but without looking at her, that he also had been very good. Then he rolled himself up in a corner while Lapino helped Mother Rabbit take the provisions out of her basket.

Soon Mother Rabbit had a nice dinner ready. Lapino ate with a fine appetite. Trottino tried to eat, too, but he could not. He felt sick. His stomach ached and his head was dizzy. At length he could bear the pain no longer. He threw himself on the ground and rolled about, uttering pitiful cries.

"What is the matter, my dear little Trottino? What is the matter, my dear child?" cried the good rabbit mother, running to him.

"Oh! dear, dear!" groaned Trottino. "I have a pain here — and here! It is like some fierce animal biting me. Oh! oh! oh!"

"What has happened to you? What have you done while I was gone? Have you eaten something poisonous?

Lapino, tell me, what is the matter?"

Lapino turned away his face. He remembered that his brother had called him a "horrid tell-tale," and he did not want to say anything.

"But there isn't anything poisonous around here," continued Mother Rabbit. "Did you go out? I distinctly forbade that!"

Both the rabbits lowered their ears with a confused air.

"You did go out? What else did you do? Did you eat anything in the meadow?"

Lapino still hesitated to speak.

TROTTINO CONFESSES.

"Not Lapino, mamma! *He* did not!" said Trottino, driven by remorse and trying to be brave.

"You only, then? What have you eaten? Tell me quickly, my poor little one. I must know in order to take care of you and cure you."

When she said this Trottino redoubled his groans. It was hard to confess, but he gasped out in broken sentences while the tears dropped from his eyes:

"We went — in a meadow. I ate — some wild thyme. Lapino didn't want me to. Oh! what a pain I have! Mamma, do help me! Do!"

"My poor little fellow! Didn't you eat anything but the wild thyme?"

"Yes — some splendid parsley. I never saw any so fine. It tasted so very good!"

"Some splendid parsley! Lapino, did *you* see it? Are you sure it was parsley?"

"I don't think it was,

mamma. I told Trottino that it was too large for parsley; and it seems to me the smell was not just the same, either"

"Unhappy child! You have mistaken *hemlock* for parsley, and it is poison! Lapino, run to the doctor and tell him that your little brother has poisoned himself. I will do the best I can for him while you are gone. But hasten, dear child, there is not a moment to be lost."

Trottino sank down in one corner quite senseless. Now and then he moaned, and moved a foot or an ear. Otherwise he seemed to be dead.

His poor mother stood over him, smoothing his head and rubbing his little paws, now one and now another, and longing for the doctor to come.

Once Trottino aroused sufficently to say again: "O, what a pain I have. Mamma, do help me! Do!"

Lapino ran as fast as he could and soon came to the house of the rabbit-doctor, who was just finishing his dinner.

The doctor wanted to give some of his dessert to Lapino, whom he knew to be a good little rabbit — very polite and well-bred; but when he was told that Trottino had poisoned himself, he quickly caught up

his hat and cane, and started out with Lapino, taking care to **carry** some medicine with him, **so** that they should not have to lose time in going to the druggist's.

They found Trottino a little better. His mother had put him to bed and given him a hot drink, then rubbed him well and covered him up warmly. But he was quite weak and ached all over, and he felt very sick indeed.

He held out his little paw to the doctor, who felt his pulse and said that he must swallow some medicine at once. Trottino drank a mouthful, but then pushed the cup away with disgust, saying, " It is nasty ! "

" What ! ' It is nasty ! ' " mimicked the doctor, in his gruffest tones. " You deserve to have it ten times as nasty, naughty, greedy child ! You must drink it right down. The sickness and the medicine are your punishment for being disobedient. Come! hurry up! you must drink it to get cured. And," he added, in a softer tone, " you

must drink it to please your poor mamma, to whom you have brought so much trouble. See! she is crying."

That decided Trottino. He took the cup and drained it to

the bottom, without making a face.

When he had finished he threw his two paws around his mother's neck, and said to her, weeping —

" Forgive me, mamma ; I will never do so any more!"

TROTTINO WELL AGAIN.

Trottino got well; and, what is better still, he was also cured of his disobedience and his greediness.

Mother Rabbit had often said to him, " Don't eat this." " Don't eat that." " It will make you sick!" but he had never really believed it. Now he knew that what she had told him was true, and he obeyed much more quickly and cheerfully than he had done before.

After his experience with the hemlock new ideas arose in Trottino's little rabbit-brain.

" There are, then," he thought, " some plants which are good to eat, and others which are dangerous, which make little rabbits sick and even make them die sometimes.

" How ought one to set about learning about these things? By tasting each plant a little and so finding out which are good and which not? But in this way one would be made sick each time he tasted of a poisonous plant. That would be terrible, that would!"

Trottino consulted his brother. Trottino often consulted Lapino.

Lapino did not know much more than Trottino, and he advised his brother not to trouble his head about such things.

But Trottino was eager to learn, so he questioned his mamma, who told him that her own mother had taught her all she knew about plants.

"And Grandmamma"—asked Trottino, "who showed her which were the good plants?"

"Her mother, my child. As long as there have been plants and rabbits, the rabbit-mothers have instructed their children; then when these children were grown up and had little rabbits of their own, they in turn taught what they had learned."

TROTTINO CONSULTS HIS MAMMA.

TROTTINO LEARNS MUCH FROM HIS MOTHER.

"And you will teach me all you know, mamma?"

"Certainly, my little one."

Trottino was delighted, and capered about with joy. Then

He "capered about with joy."

he began to help his mother about the house so that they could all go to walk sooner, and he worked just as well as Lapino.

When all was in order, they set out for a pleasant walk. As soon as they had reached the meadow, Trottino began to search out different plants and to ask questions.

"What is the name of this plant, mamma? What is the name of that? Is this good to eat? Do you think that one is poisonous?"

Mother Rabbit replied to him very patiently and told him interesting things about many of the plants which they saw; but Trottino was a little surprised to hear her sometimes answer, "I do not know." Trottino had thought that his mother knew everything. However, as he paid great attention to what she did tell him, he soon knew a great deal, for she was a well-instructed rabbit who had lived in different places where there were all sorts of plants.

Trottino had sharp eyes and

a fine sense of smell. He spied the good plants long before his mother and brother, and it was his delight to call them to share in what he found.

Indeed, it was now to be seen that Trottino was very intelligent. In a fortnight he had become more learned than his mother.

Human children have to spend a great deal more time than that in order to know as much as their mothers; but then, men and women need to learn so many more things than rabbits do.

LESSONS IN BOTANY.   TROTTINO'S EDUCATION.

"So off they all started together."

MR. GRISONNET.

Mr. Grisonnet was a wise rabbit. He was not handsome, with his gray and somewhat rough rabbit-wool, but he had a kind face and friendly ways. He was on very good terms with Lapino and Trottino, and always stopped to chat with them and their mother when he met the family in the fields.

One day as he was leaping leisurely along a hedge with his thoughts upon a rare plant which he had just been examining, he heard a voice calling to him, "Hey! Mr. Grisonnet!"

Turning about he saw Mother Rabbit at a little distance, with Lapino and Trottino at her side.

"Can you point out to us a place where there is some nice tender thyme?" said she to him. "What we find here is too old."

"Yes, come with me, neighbor; I will lead you to an excellent place," replied the old rabbit.

So off they all started together, Mr. Grisonnet and Mother Rabbit leaping gently along at a steady pace across the field, and the little ones frisking around them. Sometimes Lapino and Trottino would play a game of leapfrog

and get far ahead ; then off they would go, chasing each other, sidewise and back and all around ; and if you had tried to count them, you would have said, " There are two large rabbits, but I don't know how many little ones ! "

At last Mr. Grisonnet stopped before a beautiful bank where thyme and other herbs were thickly growing. " Ah ! what a feast," said Mother Rabbit. " Let us all enjoy it."

So each one began to nibble, taking care to thank their kind old friend for the treat he had given them. After a while, Mr. Grisonnet stopped, with a grave air, to gaze at a little plant. Trottino, who was very curious, asked him what he was looking at.

" It is a lesser centaury," replied Mr. Grisonnet. "I've never seen it about here before."

" A lesser centaury ! What a funny name ! " said Trottino. " Is it good to eat ? "

" No, it has not a good taste ; but it cures fever." Trottino opened his eyes wide.

What ! A plant which cured fever ! — Could that really be true ?

TROTTINO STUDIES WITH MR. GRISONNET.

"After all," thought Trottino, as he walked along with Mr. Grisonnet, "why should there not be plants which can cure as well as plants which can make you ill?" There were dangerous plants, like the hemlock—Trottino knew *that*, very well; and if there were others which could cure, he would be glad to know about them. So he determined to learn all he could about plants, especially those which were useful as medicine. And who could teach him better than his wise old friend, Mr. Grisonnet?

So Trottino kept close beside Mr. Grisonnet, and did not fail to notice everything that the older rabbit noticed.

Trottino would ask: "What is the name of this plant, Mr.

Grisonnet ? What is it good for ? Is it poisonous ? Does it cure fever ? "

Mr. Grisonnet was as good as he was wise. He answered Trottino's questions so carefully, and told him so much besides, that at the end of the walk Trottino had learned the names and properties of a dozen plants. In later walks he learned much more.

Rabbits grow more quickly than children. At the end of some weeks Lapino and Trottino were trusted to go about by themselves.

Good Mother Rabbit was getting older now, and became easily fatigued. She liked to stay at home, seated in her easy chair and comfortably knitting or sewing, while Lapino and Trottino went to run and play in the fields.

Often they met companions there and made happy parties. But Trottino, although he liked very much to frolic, always left his younger friends if he saw Mr. Grisonnet pass slowly by, examining plants.

In three leaps he would be

Getting older.

with him, and Mr. Grisonnet was delighted to have him as companion. Mr. Grisonnet loved to teach and Trottino to be taught, so it is no wonder that the little rabbit learned quickly. Mr. Grisonnet was continually surprised at Trottino's progress.

Mother Rabbit is ill.

TROTTINO USES HIS KNOWLEDGE.

One day Lapino and Trottino were returning home after a long walk. They were always careful to get back at the hour their mother expected them, so that she should not be anxious, and they generally found her sitting in the doorway watching for them. This time, however, there was no Mother Rabbit in sight; and as they drew nearer they heard cries which came from the back of the house. Seized with fear, they ran forward; and entering their home, found Mother Rabbit lying on the bed moaning with pain.

When she saw Lapino and Trottino she tried to rise, saying,

"Ah! my dear little ones, here you are at last. I feared I should not see you again."

The two little ones began to cry and then they asked what had happened. They saw blood on several parts of her body. The poor rabbit told them that a wicked dog had bitten her. How she ever got away from him she could not tell. She had been so frightened!

Lapino was in great grief. He loved his mother with all his little rabbit heart. He threw his paws around her neck, begging her not to die and leave them; and then he began to lick her wounds so as to ease her pain a little.

But where has Trottino gone? Does he not love his mother? Will he not try to help her, too?

Trottino had indeed gone out and left his mother, but it was with a wise and loving purpose. He now came toiling in, carrying a great bundle of herbs which he had gathered.

"Have no fear, mother," said he; "you shall not die. I have something to cure you with. Lapino, wash the parts which bleed, quickly. Oh!

you have already licked them? That is good. Then break that herb up fine." And Trottino, taking some of the same herb, mashed it up and made it into a plaster. This he placed upon the wounds. O, joy! The dear Mother

The Medicinal Herbs.

Rabbit was soon in a gentle sleep.

When she awoke, she was better; and in a few days the tender care of her children cured her. When the neighbors came to inquire after their wounded friend Lapino loved to tell them that it was Trottino — little Trottino — who had known what to do for his mother, and had brought the healing plants.

"How did the idea come to you," asked an old rabbit one day curiously, "to learn about plants which are not good to eat?"

"It is because I once poisoned myself with hemlock," replied Trottino. "That made me notice plants; so I was glad to learn about them, and dear, good Mr. Grisonnet was willing to teach me."

"But it is very plain that he has profited by other lessons as well as mine," said Mr. Grisonnet, coming up at that moment. "For instead of the once disobedient, greedy and thoughtless Trottino, we have here a good and wise little rabbit, who is a joy to his family and a credit to the rabbit race."

From the French of Madam Colomb.

MINNA'S THANKSGIVING.

A little maiden once there was
Who heard her mother say
Upon a bright November
    morn :
" This is Thanksgiving Day."

In little Minna's grateful heart
There dawned a purpose new;
" Then if this is Thanksgiving
    Day
I know what I will do."

She wrapped her in a cloak so
    warm
And tied her little hood,
And to the barn did Minna
    run
As quickly as she could.

And straight she went to
    where the cows
Stood each within its stall;
And said, and stroked their
    sides the while :
" I've come to thank you all.

" I know you give us every day
The fresh sweet milk we
    drink;
And cream and butter too, and
    cheese ;
You're *very* good, I think."

Then Minna crossed the barn,
    to speak
To Dick, the good old
    horse :

"O, Dick! when I am giving thanks
I'll thank you, too, of course.

"No matter what the time of year,
You work and work all day;
In Spring you drag the heavy plough,
In Summer loads of hay.

"You take the bags of grain to mill,
You bring the flour back;
And from the forest cart the wood,
However rough the track.

"For all these things, you dear old Dick,
I've come my thanks to pay;
I thought of it when mother said
'This is Thanksgiving Day.'"

Then down the dim and dusty barn
Did Minna trip along
To where the sheep were huddled close,
A gentle, woolly throng

She patted them with loving hand,
The sheep stood unafraid;
"Thank you for all my nice warm clothes,"
Then said the little maid.

With smiling face, and having still
Her grateful thoughts in mind,
Next to the farmyard Minna went
Her feathered friends to find.

With cluck and cackle, all the hens
Soon gathered at her feet;

Said Minna: "Thank you for
    the eggs
You've given me to eat."

Then little Minna ran again
Across the sparkling snow,
And soon was at her mother's
    side
With face and heart aglow.

"I've been and thanked them,
    mother dear,
As nicely as I could;
— The cows, the sheep, the
    hens and Dick —
I think they understood.

"For they all listened quietly
To everything I said,

And Dick! I wish you could
    have seen
The way he bowed his head.

"I'm very glad I went because
I had so much to say,
And they might all have
    thought it strange,
If I had stayed away
And had not given thanks to
    them
Upon Thanksgiving Day!"

But Minna dear, her mother
    said,
"Who gave us the animals we
    love?
Should we not be grateful to
    the Creator God above?"

"O, Yes! Indeed I almost forgot
    to thank the Lord on
    high;
For giving us our daily bread
    and Eternity by and by."

TEACHING SUGGESTIONS

Instructors are encouraged to utilize the following teaching suggestions <u>after</u> they have first read the story to their children. Use the following information to systematically review the main truths or principles contained in the stories with your students.

Section Title: Trottino - His Faults

Emphasize that <u>all</u> children are created with a sinful human nature, but that not all children have the exact same tendencies toward sin. (Some children are quiet on the outside like Lapino the rabbit, while they still struggle with rebellion and sin in their own heart.)

Remind the children that the power to resist temptation and sin comes from God the Holy Spirit - and that every true child of God has the Holy Spirit living inside their soul. Without God's help all boys and girls will grow up to be a slave to their sinful human nature. (Note John 8:31-34) Encourage your children to abandon any notion of self-sufficiency in their efforts to resist sin. Like the rabbit Trottino, children will not make real long term progress against sin without reliance upon God's Divine grace and support. Read Proverbs 3:1-6 to your students.

Point out the fact that Trottino had at least one good habit. He was willing to admit when he was wrong and ask forgiveness. Millions of youngsters never learn the importance of this Christian virtue.

Section Title: Mother Rabbit Goes to Market

Point out how Trottino cleverly tried to lie to himself regarding a supposed concern for weather as his reason for disobeying his mother. When our hearts are filled with sin any excuse for "doing what we please" will do. A sinful heart, after all, loves to deceive itself.

For example, when Trottino's brother reminded him that his mother didn't want them to go outside until they were older, Trottino responded by saying "Oh! not last week, perhaps; but we have grown since then!" Obviously, Trottino wanted to deceive himself through a series of foolish questions. Ask the children if they ever try to rationalize their disobedience by way of silly statements or questions. Warn them against the danger of self-deception and rebellion to godly authority.

Explain to the children why they should never trust the assurance of playmates who say "Come play with me. I will be good.", if the same playmates are in the midst of rebellion and sin. Read Proverbs 4:14-16. Shun evil companions is good advice for any child.

Section Title: Lapino And Trottino Stray Away

At this point in the story Trottino has become so accustomed to lying and rebellion that it is now very easy for him to sin again and again. Remind the children that one lie almost always leads to another, in cases where a person has hardened his heart and will not acknowledge the truth.

When we are lost in our own lusts, Satan always provides some kind of attractive item to encourage us in our sinful rebellion. In Trottino's life, it was a good looking basket full of lettuce, in Adam's and Eve's case it was a tree with forbidden fruit. Teach the children to be on guard against the devil's tricks and disguises. Not everything that glitters is as good as gold.

Rebellion against godly authority not only has eternal ramifications, it frequently brings pain and suffering in this present world. In Trottino's case, his attempt to steal lettuce from a neighbor lady brought him a painful kick. Remind the children of the timeless principal of Galatians 6:7; "Be not deceived; God is not mocked: for whatsoever a man soweth, that shall he also reap."

Mention at the close of this section that when we walk in obedience to God, He makes even our enemies to live in peace with us. Read Proverbs 16:7 and emphasize that the wicked have no real peace and joy in this present world.

Section Title: Trottino Eats The Poisonous Hemlock

The opening of this section finds Trottino full of anger against the women who punished him for stealing her lettuce. He should have been angry with himself and quick to repent from his wickedness. Nevertheless, he was filled with pride and a false sense of confidence. Teach children that sin blinds people from seeing their true spiritual condition. Read Hebrews 3:12-13.

Point out that Trottino did not <u>need</u> to disobey his mother and eat strange plants, for he had been given breakfast. Explain to the children that God never places an unjust temptation before any human being without also making a way of escape. Read I Corinthians 10:12-14.

Lapino had the good habit of wanting to obey his parents in <u>every</u> detail. Most youngsters are very careless and sloppy when it comes to obedience. Teach your children to follow the example of Lapino and learn to obey godly authority quickly and carefully. Read Ephesians 6:1-3.

Emphasize the truth of Ephesians 6:3 that God is often pleased to bless obedient children with long life. Trottino found out the hard way that disobedience can shorten a person's life, or at least make a person miserable! Note Proverbs 10:27.

Section Title: The Return Home

This section helps to teach children that there is a payday for sin. Trottino, however, is still resisting his conscience and trying to deny the fact that he is guilty of eating forbidden food. Help children to understand that sin can do it's greatest damage if we try to deny or suppress the truth. For example, Trottino lied to his mother when he told her that he had been good in her absence and had not eaten food outside the home. These lies could have cost him his life. Read Proverbs 28:13 to your students.

Section Title: Trottino Confesses

Trottino is finally brought to the place where he realizes the foolishness of trying to hide sins. Teach the children that Trottino's greatest mistake was trusting his wicked heart. Read Proverbs 28:26 to the students.

Encourage your students to walk in God's ways by faith and not to trust their own feelings. Remind them that sin very often looks good or feels good in the beginning. However, the end result of sin is destruction and misery. Study James 1:12-15 with the children.

Section Title: The Doctor's Visit

The doctor in this story helped Trottino put things in a proper perspective when he refused to "take his medicine." This physician reminded Trottino that he deserved ten times more punishment than he was actually getting. Help your students to understand that God does not give His children what they deserve, for <u>all</u> men are sinners and are worthy only of death and hell. God is the Great Physician who gives good gifts to the children of men by His grace - unmerited favor.

This doctor also directed Trottino to stop thinking only about himself and to realize that his wickedness has caused considerable trouble for his beloved mother. Selfishness and greed are often at the foundation of a sinful heart and produce a type of blindness regarding the needs of others. Instruct your students to appreciate the fact that a child who lives wickedly brings great sorrow to his parents. Read Proverbs 10:1 to your students.

Section Title: Trottino Well Again

Trottino learned to believe his mother's advice on what food to eat because of his experience with food poisoning. How much better it would have been for Trottino to want to obey his mother because this would please God. Remind your children that it is important to obey their parents for the right reasons. Children should not postpone obeying their parents until after they are satisfied that mom or dad can be trusted in a particular matter. Obedience is often an <u>act</u> of faith.

The wise child will follow the example of Trottino and will frequently ask his parents to instruct him in regard to the issues of life. God has given <u>all</u> parents the duty to be teachers to their children. (Note Proverbs 1:1-9 and 22:26) Encourage the children to get into the good habit of seeking advice and instruction from their parents.

Section Title: Trottino Learns Much From His Mother

The home is the first and most basic school of life. Children have a duty to use the mind and talents that God has provided to seek out knowledge and wisdom. Encourage the students to look at learning as a life-long duty. Youngsters need to take advantage of every opportunity God provides to gain wisdom. (Note Proverbs 5:1-13)

Section Titles: Mr. Grisonnet and Trottino Studies With Mr. Grisonnet

These two sections can help children understand the value of old people and the responsibility that youngsters have to honor godly men and women who are in their old age. Point out the many things that young children can learn from people who have lived a long time. Also emphasize that the main reason why Trottino learned so much from older people was because of his attitude - he was eager to learn. Remind your children that this attitude is pleasing to God.

Share the following Bible passage with your students in an effort to encourage them to honor and respect senior citizens who are godly. (Proverbs 16:31) Balance this teaching by instructing children that they should not expect their parents or other adults to know everything. Only God is infinite in wisdom. You could use the example from Job 32:4-10, to show that even great and wise men like Job were not always wise. Children need to realize that they have a God-given duty to respect their elders regardless of whether those elders can answer every question under the sun.

Section Title: Trottino Uses His Knowledge

Point out in this final section that God is pleased when older children help to care for their aging parents. Also, emphasize that children often learn things when they are very young that come in very handy many years later. Trottino for example, learned all about herbs and plants years before he ever needed this knowledge to help his aged mother. Remind children that the knowledge and wisdom they gain in their youth will permit them to be more useful as a servant of God when they are older.

Close by teaching the children that the greatest knowledge that anyone can find is the knowledge of God's love and grace. Read Proverbs 8:32-36.

MINNA'S THANKSGIVING

The main point to emphasize from this story is that God is the one who is ultimately responsible for giving us all things to enjoy. James 1:17 states, "Every good gift and every perfect gift is from above, and cometh down from the Father of lights, with whom is no variableness, neither shadow of turning." Therefore, more that any mere creature, God deserves all the glory that thankful hearts can render for great things He hath done!

One additional point is worth mentioning to your students. Teach your youngsters to praise God for who He is, and not just for what He does for mankind. After all, John 17:5, makes it clear that God the Father and God the Son were glorified before the world began.

The Lord would be worthy of our praise and adoration even if He never created a wonderful world or saved a guilty soul. Far too often, we permit our attitude of gratitude to slip away because we perceive that God is not giving us all the physical blessings we think we deserve. This lack of thankfulness, during times of spiritual testing, often results from the foolish notion that God is not worthy of our praise unless He is showering us with gifts. The following poem helps to shed a proper perspective on the subject of thankfulness. Please share this poem with your students.

HYMN OF THANKSGIVING

For the blessings of the field,
For the stores the gardens yield,
For the vine's exalted juice,
For the generous olive's use;

Flocks that whiten all the plain,
Yellow sheaves of ripened grain,
Clouds that drop their fattening dews,
Suns that temperate warmth diffuse;

All that Spring, with bounteous hand,
Scatters o'er the smiling land;
All that liberal Autumn pours
From her rich o'erflowing stores;

These to Thee, my God, we owe--
Source whence all our blessings flow!
And for these my soul shall raise
Grateful vows and solemn praise.

Yet should rising whirlwinds tear
From its stem the ripening ear,
Should the fig tree's blasted shoot
Drop her green untimely fruit--

Should the vine put forth no more,
Nor the olive yield her store,
Though the sickening flocks should fall,
And the herds desert the stall--

Should thine altered hand restrain
The early and the latter rain,
Blast each opening bud of joy,
And the rising year destroy--

Yet to Thee my soul should raise
Grateful vows and solemn praise,
And, when every blessing's flown,
Love Thee - for Thyself alone.

Anna Loetitla Barbauld